THE WONDER THING

by Libby Hathorn
illustrated by Peter Gouldthorpe

Houghton Mifflin Company
Boston New York
1996

For my mother

L. H.

For Lucy and Oliver

P. G.

Text copyright © 1995 by Libby Hathorn
Illustrations copyright © 1995 by Peter Gouldthorpe

First American edition 1996 published by Houghton Mifflin Company
First published in Australia by Penguin Books Australia Ltd.

For information about this and other Houghton Mifflin trade and reference books
and multimedia products, visit The Bookstore at Houghton Mifflin
on the World Wide Web at (http://www. hmco.com/trade/).

Manufactured in Australia by Southbank Book
The text of this book is set in 21-point Bembo semibold.
10 9 8 7 6 5 4 3 2 1

Library of Congress Cataloging-in-Publication Data
Hathorn, Elizabeth.
The wonder thing / by Libby Hathorn ; illustrated by Peter Gouldthorpe.—
1st American ed.
p.   cm.
ISBN 0-395-71541-5
1. Water — Juvenile literature. [1. Water.] I. Gouldthorpe, Peter, ill.
II. Title.
GB662.3.H38   1996   551.48—dc20   94-19912   CIP   AC

High above the peaks

On the wild mountainto

Deep underground

In the swirling mist

Under the melting snow

Down the sheer mountainside

Over the riverbeds

Through the lilting rainforests

And still afternoons

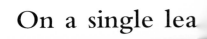

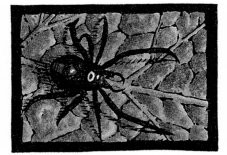

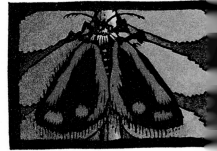

n the rotting mulch

Among the glowing fungi

Through billowing grasslands

And the trackless swamp

Out in the tangy sea

In the smallest village

And the largest town

Good as gold

Precious as air

Powerful as rocl

Gentle as kisses

Lovely as life is

For the life it will bring

Splendid as rainbow

A miracle thing

WATER